THE LOUD HOUSE

LOVE OUT LOUD

LOVE OUT LOUD

"PUPPY LOVE"
Kiernan Sjursen-Lien — Writer
D.K. Terrell — Artist, Colorist
Wilson Ramos Jr. — Letterer

"SIR RIBBIT"
Rebecca E. Banks — Writer
Amanda Tran — Artist, Colorist
Wilson Ramos Jr. — Letterer

"SIBLING APPRECIATION DAY"
Kara Fein — Writer
Zazo Aguiar— Artist, Colorist
Wilson Ramos Jr. — Letterer

"TIME TO RHYME"
Kiernan Sjursen-Lien — Writer
Amanda Tran — Artist, Colorist
Wilson Ramos Jr. — Letterer

"TWEETHEARTS"
Jair Holguin — Writer
Daniela Rodriguez — Artist, Colorist
Wilson Ramos Jr. — Letterer

"HAPPY PLAN-IVERSARY"
Kara Fein — Writer
Erin Hyde — Artist, Colorist
Wilson Ramos Jr. — Letterer

"WHAT'S LOVE GOT TO DO WITH IT?"
Paloma Uribe — Writer
Amanda Tran — Artist, Colorist
Wilson Ramos Jr. — Letterer

"BEAR HUG"
Amanda Fein — Writer
Daniela Rodriguez — Artist, Colorist
Wilson Ramos Jr. — Letterer

"CUPID'S WINGS"
Kara Fein — Writer
Melissa Kleynowski— Artist
Amanda Tran — Colorist
Wilson Ramos Jr. — Letterer

"BOA ON BOARD"
Amanda Fein — Writer
Zazo Aguiar — Penciller, Colorist
Karolyn Rocha — Inker
Wilson Ramos Jr. — Letterer

"FOR THE LOVE OF THE GAME"
Amanda Fein — Writer
D.K. Terrell — Artist, Colorist
Wilson Ramos Jr. — Letterer

"CAFÉ CONFUSION"
Caitlin Fein — Writer
Max Alley — Artist
Peter Bertucci — Colorist
Wilson Ramos Jr. — Letterer

"OVER THE LINE"
Amanda Fein — Writer
Shannon Parayil — Artist, Colorist
Wilson Ramos Jr. — Letterer

"MANIC MONDAY"
Jair Holguin — Writer
Lena Bishop — Layout Artist
Melissa Kleynowski — Inker
Efrain Rodriguez — Colorist
Wilson Ramos Jr. — Letterer

"MADE WITH CARE"
Derek Fridolfs — Writer
D.K. Terrell — Artist, Colorist
Wilson Ramos Jr. — Letterer

"FROM THE HEART"
Kara Fein — Writer
Melissa Kleynowski — Artist
Efrain Rodriguez — Colorist
Wilson Ramos Jr. — Letterer

"SENIOR PROM"
Amanda Fein — Writer
Zazo Aguiar — Penciller, Colorist
Karolyn Rocha — Inker
Wilson Ramos Jr. — Letterer

"THERE'S SOMETHING ABOUT LALO"
Amanda Fein — Writer
Jennifer Hernandez — Artist, Colorist
Wilson Ramos Jr. — Letterer

"O-PUN-ING NIGHT"
Jair Holguin — Writer
Michelle Hiraishi — Artist, Colorist
Wilson Ramos Jr. — Letterer

"FRIENDIVERSARY"
Jair Holguin — Writer
Erin Hyde — Artist, Colorist
Wilson Ramos Jr. — Letterer

TYLER KOBERSTEIN — Cover Artist
JORDAN ROSATO — Endpapers
JAMES SALERNO — Sr. Art Director/Nickelodeon
JAYJAY JACKSON — Design
EMMA BONE, CAITLIN FEIN, KRISTEN G. SMITH, NEIL WADE, DANA CLUVERIUS, MOLLIE FREILICH — Special Thanks
JORDAN HILLMAN — Editorial Intern
JEFF WHITMAN — Editor
JOAN HILTY — Comics Editor/Nickelodeon
JIM SALICRUP
Editor-in-Chief

ISBN: 978-1-5458-0854-2 paperback edition
ISBN: 978-1-5458-0853-5 hardcover edition

Papercutz books may be purchased for business or promotional use. For information on bulk purchases please contact Macmillan Corporate and Premium Sales Department at (800) 221-7945 x5442.

Printed in Turkey
December 2021

Distributed by Macmillan
First Printing

MEET THE LOUD FAMILY
and friends!

LINCOLN LOUD
THE MIDDLE CHILD

Lincoln is the middle child, with five older sisters and five younger sisters. He has learned that surviving the Loud household means staying a step ahead. He's the man with a plan, always coming up with a way to get what he wants or deal with a problem, even if things inevitably go wrong. Being the only boy comes with some perks. Lincoln gets his own room – even if it's just a converted linen closet. On the other hand, being the only boy also means he sometimes gets a little too much attention from his sisters. They mother him, tease him, and use him as the occasional lab rat or fashion show participant. Lincoln's sisters may drive him crazy, but he loves them and is always willing to help out if they need him.

LORI LOUD
THE OLDEST

As the first-born child of the Loud Clan, Lori sees herself as the boss of all her siblings. She feels she's paved the way for them and deserves extra respect. Her signature traits are rolling her eyes, texting her boyfriend, Bobby, and literally saying "literally" all the time. Because she's the oldest and most experienced sibling, Lori can be a great ally, so it pays to stay on her good side, especially since she can drive.

LENI LOUD
THE FASHIONISTA

Leni spends most of her time designing outfits and accessorizing. She always falls for Luan's pranks, and sometimes walks into walls when she's talking (she's not great at doing two things at once). Leni might be flighty, but she's the sweetest of the Loud siblings and truly has a heart of gold (even though she's pretty sure it's a heart of blood).

LUNA LOUD
THE ROCK STAR

Luna is loud, boisterous and freewheeling, and her energy is always cranked to 11. She thinks about music so much that she even talks in song lyrics. On the off-chance she doesn't have her guitar with her, everything can and will be turned into a musical instrument. You can always count on Luna to help out, and she'll do most anything you ask, as long as you're okay with her supplying a rocking guitar accompaniment.

LUAN LOUD
THE JOKESTER

Luan's a standup comedienne who provides a nonstop barrage of silly puns. She's big on prop comedy too – squirting flowers and whoopee cushions – so you have to be on your toes whenever she's around. She loves to pull pranks and is a really good ventriloquist – she is often found doing bits with her dummy, Mr. Coconuts. Luan never lets anything get her down; to her, laughter IS the best medicine.

LYNN LOUD
THE ATHLETE

Lynn is athletic and full of energy and is always looking for a teammate. With her, it's all sports all the time. She'll turn anything into a sport. Putting away eggs? Jump shot! Score! Cleaning up the eggs? Slap shot! Score! Lynn is very competitive, but despite her competitive nature, she always tries to just have a good time.

LUCY LOUD
THE EMO

You can always count on Lucy to give the morbid point of view in any given situation. She is obsessed with all things spooky and dark – funerals, vampires, séances, and the like. She wears mostly black and writes moody poetry. She's usually quiet and keeps to herself. Lucy has a way of mysteriously appearing out of nowhere, and try as they might, her siblings never get used to this.

LOLA LOUD
THE BEAUTY QUEEN

Lola could not be more different from her twin sister, Lana. She's a pageant powerhouse whose interests include glitter, photo shoots, and her own beautiful, beautiful face. But don't let her cute, gap-toothed smile fool you; underneath all the sugar and spice lurks a Machiavellian mastermind. Whatever Lola wants, Lola gets – or else. She's the eyes and ears of the household and never resists an opportunity to tattle on troublemakers. But if you stay on Lola's good side, you've got yourself a fierce ally – and a lifetime supply of free makeovers.

LANA LOUD
THE TOMBOY

Lana is the rough-and-tumble sparkplug counterpart to her twin sister, Lola. She's all about reptiles, mud pies, and muffler repair. She's the resident Ms. Fix-it and is always ready to lend a hand – the dirtier the job, the better. Need your toilet unclogged? Snake fed? Back-zit popped? Lana's your gal. All she asks in return is a little A-B-C gum, or a handful of kibble (she often sneaks it from the dog bowl).

LISA LOUD
THE GENIUS

Lisa is smarter than the rest of her siblings combined. She'll most likely be a rocket scientist, or a brain surgeon, or an evil genius who takes over the world. Lisa spends most of her time working in her lab (the family has gotten used to the explosions), and says her research leaves little time for frivolous human pursuits like "playing" or "getting haircuts." That said, she's always there to help with a homework question, or to explain why the sky is blue, or to point out the structural flaws in someone's pillow fort. Lisa says it's the least she can do for her favorite test subjects, er, siblings.

LILY LOUD
THE BABY

Lily is a giggly, drooly, diaper-ditching free spirit, affectionately known as "the poop machine." You can't keep a nappy on this kid – she's like a teething Houdini. But even when Lily's running wild, dropping rancid diaper bombs, or drooling all over the remote, she always brings a smile to everyone's face (and a clothespin to their nose). Lily is everyone's favorite little buddy, and the whole family loves her unconditionally.

RITA LOUD

Mother to the eleven Loud kids, Mom (Rita Loud) wears many different hats. She's a chauffeur, homework-checker and barf-cleaner-upper all rolled into one. She's always there for her kids and ready to jump into action during a crisis, whether it's a fight between the twins or Leni's missing shoe. When she's not chasing the kids around or at her day job as a dental hygienist, Mom pursues her passion: writing. She also loves taking on house projects and is very handy with tools (guess that's where Lana gets it from). Between writing, working and being a mom, her days are always hectic but she wouldn't have it any other way.

LYNN LOUD SR.

Dad (Lynn Loud Sr.) is a fun-loving, upbeat aspiring chef. A kid-at-heart, he's not above taking part in the kids' zany schemes. In addition to cooking, Dad loves his van, playing the cowbell and making puns. Before meeting Mom, Dad spent a semester in England and has been obsessed with British culture ever since – and sometimes "accidentally" slips into a British accent. When Dad's not wrangling the kids, he's pursuing his dream of opening his own restaurant where he hopes to make his "Lynn-sagnas" world-famous.

CHARLES

WALT

CLIFF

GEO

POP POP

Albert, the Loud kids' grandfather, currently lives at Sunset Canyon Retirement Community after dedicating his life to working in the military. Pop Pop spends his days dominating at shuffleboard, eating pudding, and going on adventures with his pals Bernie, Scoots, and Seymour and his girlfriend, Myrtle. Pop Pop is upbeat, fun-loving, and cherishes spending time with his grandchildren.

MYRTLE

Myrtle, or Gran-Gran, is Albert's (Pop Pop's) girlfriend. She loves traveling and hanging out with Albert and the Loud kids. Since she doesn't have grandkids of her own, she's the Loud kids' honorary grandma and can't help but smother them with love.

CLYDE McBRIDE
THE BEST FRIEND

Clyde is Lincoln's partner in crime. He's always willing to go along with Lincoln's crazy schemes (even if he sees the flaws in them up-front). Lincoln and Clyde are two peas in a pod and share pretty much all of the same tastes in movies, comics, TV shows, toys—you name it. As an only child, Clyde envies Lincoln—how cool would it be to always have siblings around to talk to? But since Clyde spends so much time at the Loud household, he's almost an honorary sibling anyway.

HAROLD AND HOWARD McBRIDE
Clyde's Loving Dads

Harold and Howard are Clyde's loving dads and only want the best for him, but what they define as "the best" may differ. Harold is a level-headed, straight-shooter with a heart of gold. The more easygoing of Clyde's dads, Harold often has to convince Howard that it's okay for them to not constantly hover over Clyde. Howard is an anxious helicopter parent and it's easy for him to break down into emotional sobbing, whether it be sad times (like when Clyde stubbed his toe) or happy (like when Clyde and Lincoln beat that really tough video game boss). Despite their differing parenting styles, the two dads bring nothing but love to the table.

CLEOPAWTRA
Clyde's Cat

NEPURRTITI
Clyde's Other Cat

BENNY STEIN

Benny is Luan's classmate, costar, and boyfriend. He's shy and quirky, but also sweet and earnest. He's not a zany comedian like Luan, but he sure enjoys her sense of humor and appreciates her wicked skills when it comes to prop comedy. Luan keeps Benny laughing, and Benny keeps Luan from sweating the small stuff. And as his marionette, Mrs. Appleblossom, would remind him (in her sassy British accent), it's all small stuff.

SAM SHARP

Sam is Luna's classmate and good friend, who Luna has a crush on. Sam is all about the music – she loves to play guitar and write and compose music. Her favorite genre is rock and roll but she appreciates all good tunes. Unlike Luna, Sam only has one brother, Simon, but she thinks even one sibling provides enough chaos for her.

RONNIE ANNE SANTIAGO

Ronnie Anne's a skateboarding city girl now. She's fearless, free-spirited, and always quick to come up with a plan. She's one tough cookie, but she also has a sweet side. Ronnie Anne loves helping her family, and that's taught her to help others, too. When she's not pitching in at the family mercado, you can find her exploring the neighborhood with her best friend Sid, or ordering hot dogs with her skater buds Casey, Nikki, and Sameer.

BOBBY SANTIAGO

Bobby is Ronnie Anne's big bro. He's a student and one of the hardest workers in the city! He loves his family and loves working at the Mercado. As his Abuelo's right hand man, Bobby can't wait to take over the family business one day. He's a big kid at heart, and his clumsiness gets him into some sticky situations at work, like locking himself in the freezer. Mercado mishaps aside, everyone in the neighborhood loves to come to the store and talk to Bobby.

MARIA CASAGRANDE SANTIAGO

She's the mother of Bobby and Ronnie Anne. A hardworking nurse, she doesn't get to spend a lot of time with her kids, but when she does she treasures it. Maria is calm and rational but often worries about whether she's doing enough for her kids. Maria, Bobby, and Ronnie Anne are a close-knit trio who were used to having only each other – until they moved in with their extended family.

SERGIO

Sergio is the Casagrandes' beloved pet parrot. He's a blunt, sassy bird who "thinks" he's full of wisdom and always has something to say. The Casagrandes have to keep a close eye on their credit card as Sergio is addicted to online shopping and is always asking the family to buy him some new gadget he saw on TV. Sergio is most loyal to Rosa and serves as her wing-man, partner in crime, taste tester, and confidant. He can be found trying to get his ex-girlfriend, Priscilla (an ostrich at the zoo), to respond to him.

HECTOR CASAGRANDE

Hector is Carlos and Maria's dad, and the Abuelo of the family (that means grandpa)! He owns the Mercado on the ground floor of their apartment building and takes great pride in his work, his family, and being the unofficial "mayor" of the block. He loves to tell stories, share his ideas, and gossip (even though he won't admit it). You can find him working in the Mercado, playing guitar, or watching his favorite telenovela.

ROSA CASAGRANDE

Rosa is Carlos and Maria's mom and the Abuela of the family (that means grandma)! She's the head of the household, the wisest Casagrande, and the master cook with a superhuman ability to tell when anyone in the house is hungry. She often tries to fix problems or illnesses with traditional Mexican home remedies and potions. She's very protective of her family... sometimes a little too much.

CARLOS CASAGRANDE

Carlos is Maria's brother. He's married to Frida, and together they have four kids: Carlota, C.J., Carl, and Carlitos. Carlos is a Professor of Cultural Studies at a local college. Usually he has his heads in the clouds or his nose in a textbook. Relatively easygoing, Carlos is a loving father and an enthusiastic teacher who tries to get his kids interested in their Mexican heritage.

FRIDA PUGA CASAGRANDE

Frida is Carlos, C.J., Carl, and Carlitos' mom. She's an art professor and a performance artist, and is always looking for new ways to express herself. She's got a big heart and isn't shy about her emotions. Frida tends to cry when she's sad, happy, angry, or any other emotion you can think of. She's always up for fun, is passionate about her art, and loves her family more than anything.

CARLOTA CASAGRANDE

Carlota is CJ, Carl, and Carlitos' older sister. A social media influencer, she's excited to be like a big sister to Ronnie Anne. She's a force to be reckoned with, and is always trying to share her distinctive vintage style tips with Ronnie Anne.

CARLITOS CASAGRANDE

Carlitos is the baby of the family, and is always copying the behavior of everyone in the household—even if they aren't human. He's a playful and silly baby who loves to play with the family pets.

CJ (CARLOS JR.) CASAGRANDE

CJ is Carlota's younger brother and Carl and Carlitos' older brother. He was born with Down Syndrome. He lights up any room with his infectious smile and is always ready to play. He's obsessed with pirates and is BFFs with Bobby. He likes to wear a bowtie to any family occasion, and you can always catch him laughing or helping his *abuela*.

CARL CASAGRANDE

Carl is wise beyond his years. He's confident, outgoing, and puts a lot of time and effort into looking good. He likes to think of himself as a suave businessman and doesn't like to get caught playing with his action figures or wearing his footie PJs. Even though Bobby is nothing but nice to him, Carl sees his big cousin as his biggest rival.

LALO

Lalo is a slobbery bull mastiff who thinks he's a lapdog. He's not the smartest pup, and gets scared easily… but he loves his family and loves to cuddle.

STANLEY CHANG

Stanley Chang is Sid's dad. He's a conductor on the GLART-train that runs through the city. He's a patient man who likes to do Tai Chi when he gets stressed out. He likes to cheer up train commuters with fun facts, but emotionally he breaks down more than the train does.

BECCA CHANG

Becca Chang is Sid's mom. Like her daughter, Becca is quirky, smart, and funny. She works at the Great Lakes City Zoo and often brings her work home with her, which means the Chang household can also be a bit of a zoo.

ADELAIDE CHANG

Adelaide Chang is Sid's little sister. She's 6 years old, and has a flair for the dramatic. You can always find her trying to make her way into her big sister Sid's adventures.

FROGGY 2

SID CHANG

Sid is Ronnie Anne's quirky best friend. She's new to the city but dives head-first into everything she finds interesting. She and her family just moved into the apartment one floor above the Casagrandes. In fact, Sid's bedroom is right above Ronnie Anne's! A dream come true for any BFFs.

MAYBELLE

Maybelle is a cranky neighborhood regular at the *Mercado* who is obsessed with mangoes. They might be the only thing she eats! Her other loves include movie heartthrob Javier Luna and a good deal. Maybelle is very picky and never misses a chance to complain, but the Casagrandes love her dearly.

"PUPPY LOVE"

"SIBLING APPRECIATION DAY"

"TWEETHEARTS"

"WHAT'S LOVE GOT TO DO WITH IT?"

21

"CUPID'S WINGS"

END

23

"FOR THE LOVE OF THE GAME"

"OVER THE LINE"

27

"MADE WITH CARE"

29

31

"O-PUN-ING NIGHT"

"SIR RIBBIT"

"TIME TO RHYME"

40

"HAPPY PLAN-IVERSARY"

"BEAR HUG"

47

49

50

"FROM THE HEART"

AYE, **CARLITOS!** THIS SCARF ALREADY HAS STAINS ON IT FROM WHEN YOU SPILLED MY HOMEMADE QUESO...

...AND NOW ALL THIS DROOL!

⸖GIGGLE!⸖

I WILL SURPRISE **ROSA** WITH THE MOST BEAUTIFUL HAND-MADE SCARF, **LALO!**

WOOF!

⸖HMPH!⸖ THIS MIGHT BE HARDER THAN I THOUGHT.

I CAN TAKE CARE OF THE **MERCADO**, **ABUELO**. MAYBE **CARLOTA** CAN HELP YOU?

GOOD IDEA, **ROBERTO**. SHE KNOWS FASHION.

SPECIAL ICE CREAM 49¢

WATCH **THIS** VIDEO ON CROSS-STITCHING, THIS VIDEO ON HOW TO MAKE A SCARF IN 10 MINUTES, AND **THIS** ONE ON SCARF FASHION THROUGH THE AGES!

MAKE A SCARF WITH ME! (LIVE) Cross-stitch the perfect scarf! 232 watch

SPECIALTY YARN SALE

Scarf-MANIA! The Scarf Source: Scarf Fashion Through The Ages! 1,359 views

⸖GAH!⸖ THIS IS MAKING ME HUNGRY. I NEED BRAIN FOOD TO GET THROUGH ALL THESE VIDEOS.

GRUMBLE

"FRIENDIVERSARY"

*SEE THE LOUD HOUSE #12'S "OLLIE, OLLIE OXEN FREE"

*SEE CASAGRANDES #1'S "FOR A FEW TICKETS MORE"

WATCH OUT FOR PAPERCUTZ ™

Welcome to THE LOUD HOUSE extra-special, extra-lovable graphic novel "Love Out Loud," from Papercutz, those love-sick souls dedicated to publishing great graphic novels for all ages. I'm Jim Salicrup, Editor-in-Chief and Hopeless Romantic, here to talk about love, Loud-style.

While this special edition of THE LOUD HOUSE is obviously built around the wonderful theme of love, the truth is that you can find examples of love in every volume of THE LOUD HOUSE graphic novels and on the Nickelodeon TV series as well. I'm not just talking about the various characters that are part of couples who are in love with each other, but the love the Loud family clearly has for each other and for their many friends. And it's a good thing that they're so loving—it's difficult enough for most average-sized families to get along, for a family with eleven children, as many of the stories in this graphic novel illustrate, it's quite a challenge!

While we often see those challenges played out here and on TV, one of the reasons things usually work out so well for the Loud family is the love and respect they have for each other. Clearly each child has had the freedom to pursue their own special interests with nothing but love and support coming from their parents, relatives, and friends. What a truly wonderful environment in which to grow up. Everyone is free to be exactly who they want to be, and they're accepted and loved. The same is true for THE CASAGRANDES as well.

I can only hope and wish that everyone who enjoys THE LOUD HOUSE is equally lucky in their lives. Unfortunately, we know that in the real world things are not always quite as wonderful as we wish they were. It's important for each of us to remember that and to do our best to treat everyone like we would like to be treated. It's not always easy, but sometimes just a little bit of kindness can go a long way. For

example, if you know someone else who loves THE LOUD HOUSE as much as you, you might offer to share this very graphic novel with that person. It's fun to have a common interest with a friend or family member. It's great to see fans of THE LOUD HOUSE discuss the latest episodes and graphic novels online—even when individuals disagree about specific bits, they're still bound together with a shared love for THE LOUD HOUSE.

While the priority for the creators of THE LOUD HOUSE cartoons and comics is to provide entertaining stories that we hope will make you laugh, we also hope that while you're enjoying THE LOUD HOUSE you also feel the love and know that you're loved too.

Love is love.

Thanks,

Jim

We have two special bonuses that you are sure to love! First, a look at Tyler Kobertstein's creative process putting together the cover for this very volume! Then, a callback to the origins of the Friendiversary, all the way back in ninth THE LOUD HOUSE graphic novel! Enjoy!

STAY IN TOUCH!

EMAIL: salicrup@papercutz.com
WEB: papercutz.com
TWITTER: @papercutzgn
INSTAGRAM: @papercutzgn
FACEBOOK: PAPERCUTZGRAPHICNOVELS
FANMAIL: Papercutz, 160 Broadway, Suite 700, East Wing, New York, NY 10038

Go to papercutz.com and sign up for the free Papercutz e-newsletter!

"THE PERFECT GIFT"

Katie Mattila — Writer • Max Alley — Artist • JayJay Jackson— Colorist • Wilson Ramos Jr. — Letterer